Guy Parker-Rees

DYLAN

THE TEACHER

Hello, I'm Dotty Bug. Let's join in with the story!

When it's a sunny day,
Dylan's ready to play.
But what kind of day
was it today?

A stay-at-home, don't-learn-anything kind of day?

No way!

"Today," said Dylan, "is a day for being a teacher, so that I can teach my friends all the things I know."

What's under YOUR bed?

Dylan dived under his bed, rummaged around, and found . . .

. . . a big heavy school bell.

He set up his classroom, and put on some glasses to make himself look extra clever.
"What else do I need?" thought Dylan. "Oh, yes! I need someone to teach!"

Dylan clanged his heavy school bell.

Ding-a-ling-a-ling!

All his friends came running to see what the noise was.
"School time!" shouted Dylan. "Everyone come into the classroom!"

"Now settle down, class, and pay attention to me!" said Dylan.

Have YOU ever sat in a classroom?

Titchy Chick was a bit worried about going to school, so
she snuggled up close to Purple Puss. Jolly Otter put up his hand.
"What's the first lesson, Dylan?"

Oh, dear.
Dylan hadn't thought
about that.

He scratched his head,
but he couldn't think
of anything.

"I know!" said Purple Puss.
"I could teach everyone
how to climb trees."

"I'm the teacher!"
said Dylan. "Follow me, and
I'll teach you how to climb trees!"

Dylan clanged his bell,

ding-a-ling-a-ling!

and marched them all to
the big climbing tree in the woods.

Do YOU like climbing trees?

But Dylan wasn't very
good at climbing trees.
"Help!" he said. "I'm stuck!"

Everyone had to help him down.
"What's our next lesson, Dylan?"
said Purple Puss.

"I know!" said Jolly Otter. "Titchy Chick
could teach us all how to skip."

"I'm the teacher!" said Dylan.
"Follow me, and I'll teach
you all how to skip!"
He clanged his bell,

Would YOU like to live in
Titchy Chick's house?

ding-a-ling-a-ling!

and marched them all to Titchy Chick's
house, to find some skipping ropes.

Titchy Chick could skip very well,
but everyone else found it tricky.

Purple Puss's tail kept
getting in the way,

Jolly Otter kept falling over,
and Dylan couldn't do it at all.

Have YOU ever
tried skipping?

It took ages
to untangle him.

"What's our next lesson, Dylan?" said Purple Puss.
"I know!" said Jolly Otter. "I could teach everyone
how to paddle my boat."

"I'm the teacher!" said Dylan.
"Follow me, and I'll teach you how to paddle a boat!"

He clanged his bell, ding-a-ling-a-ling!
and marched them all to Jolly Otter's boat by the river.

They all climbed in and Dylan stood up.
"Now pay attention, everyone!"

But before he could teach them
anything, the boat started to wobble.
"I don't think you should stand up in
the boat, Dylan," said Jolly Otter.

But it was too late.

Look out!

Everyone was soggy and grumpy.

"Perhaps you should just teach things that
you know about," said Purple Puss.

Dylan was very sad.
"I wanted to teach **something**
but I'm no good at teaching
anything!"

And he stomped away.

Come back,
Dylan!

But all that stomping gave him an idea.
"I know what the next lesson is!" he said.

What do YOU think Dylan is going to teach next?

"Pay attention, class, and do what I do! I'm going to teach you my special Cheery-Warm-Up Dance."

No one was very keen.
But then Dylan started to sing . . .

"STOMP like an elephant,

WIGGLE like a worm,

Flap like an eagle and

turn turn turn.

"Stretch
like a grizzly bear,

Can YOU
join in, too?

hop
like
a flea!

ROAR
like a lion,

But you won't
catch me!"

Dylan ran off, ringing his bell as loud as he could.
The whole class roared like lions
and chased after him . . .

. . . all the way back to the school.

What would YOU teach?

"Caught you!" said Jolly Otter.
And they all fell on top of him, laughing.

"I like school," said Titchy Chick.
"Can I come again tomorrow?"
"Yes," said Dylan. "Who wants to be teacher?"

First published in the UK in 2017 by
Alison Green Books
An imprint of Scholastic Children's Books
Euston House, 24 Eversholt Street
London NW1 1DB
A division of Scholastic Ltd
www.scholastic.co.uk
London – New York – Toronto – Sydney – Auckland
Mexico City – New Delhi – Hong Kong

HB ISBN: 978 1 40717173 9
PB ISBN: 978 1 40717174 6

1 3 5 7 9 8 6 4 2

To Ann Jungman,
my inspirational Primary School teacher,
and all you teachers out there.